To the Edge of the World

A Story About Alexander the Great

Stewart Ross

Illustrated by Bob Moulder

an imprint of Hodder Children's Books

Alexander the Great (356-323BC)

356 BC Alexander (later known as Alexander the Great) was born in Macedonia, a kingdom in northern Greece. His father was King Philip II, his mother Queen Olympias.

336 Philip II was killed and Alexander came to the throne of Macedonia, aged nineteen.

335-4 Alexander defeated rebels at home and conquered the territory surrounding Macedonia. At Granicus he won his first battle against the Persians, the strongest power in the region.

333-30 Now king of a great empire, Alexander conquered the Middle East, including Egypt. He then invaded Persia and became Lord of All Asia.

329-8 Alexander's empire spread east to the Himalayan mountains. Having defeated the warlike people of Sogdiana, Alexander married Roxana, a beautiful princess of that region.

323 After the Battle of Hydaspes, Alexander advanced further east. At the River Beas, believing they were near the edge of the world, his men refused to go any further. Some of them returned home by sea. The rest, led by the king himself, fought their way back to Babylon in modern Iraq. Here, Alexander was taken ill during a great feast. He died eleven days later and his generals divided his empire between them.

Chapter 1
Lord of All Asia

'Strange place for a wedding,' said Ariam, gazing up at the castle-topped pinnacle of grey rock known as Koh-i-noor.

Baron Pitames put a friendly arm around his eleven-year-old son's shoulders. 'Careful, Ariam. It's not a good idea to question the Lord of All Asia. They say he's a god, you know. He has probably chosen Koh-i-noor so he can look down on ordinary mortals.'

Ariam smiled. He looked older than his age and liked it when his father talked to him like an adult. 'Do you really think Alexander is a god, Father?' he asked.

'I don't know,' the baron replied. 'But anyone who has conquered the Persians, Parthians, Sogdians and goodness knows who else is no ordinary man.'

As they continued up the steep path towards the castle, Ariam thought over his father's words. Of course Alexander was no ordinary man. Only a military genius could have captured Koh-i-noor. And only a handsome hero could have won the heart of Ariam's cousin Roxana, the most beautiful woman in Asia.

By the time they reached the castle, Ariam had built up an image of Alexander as a huge, heroic warrior. He couldn't wait to see him.

Roxana, the 'Little Star', sat as still as
stone on a painted throne at the far end of
the hall. Her silvery dress glinted in the
light of a hundred flaming torches.
Shimmering silk veiled her face. She looks
like a queen already, thought Ariam. Only
the occasional twitching of her fingers
betrayed her nervousness.

Beside her, dressed in scarlet robes, stood her father, Baron Oxyartes, Ariam's uncle. Guests thronged the hall: close-cropped, square-shouldered Macedonian soldiers, nobles from Sogdiana and Bactria, Persian gentlemen, Greek teachers, half-naked servants and even a prince from distant India.

As Ariam was wondering whether the Indian had ridden to Koh-i-noor on an elephant, trumpets sounded and the doors at the end of the hall were thrown open. Everyone except the Greeks bowed their heads. Lifting his eyes, Ariam saw a short man walk quickly into the room. His hair was longer than the soldiers' and he wore Persian clothes. Ariam glanced towards the entrance to see if the king was following. The doors had been closed.

Suddenly, Ariam realized his mistake. The man striding briskly down the hall towards Roxana was not a Persian. He was Alexander of Macedonia, Lord of All Asia, the most powerful king in the world.

Chapter 2
'Who Are You?'

Ariam was too young to join in the three days of feasting that followed the marriage ceremony. Even so, he found plenty of opportunity to study the famous soldier-king.

Alexander was truly an amazing man. His small size seemed to add to his power: he was like a firefly, all darting energy and flashing eyes.

There was nothing he couldn't do. He drank wine all night with the Macedonians. In the morning, fresh as dew, he exchanged ideas in different languages with the court philosophers. After an afternoon of hunting, he talked tactics with his generals before joining Roxana for the evening feast. On and on he went, never tiring, always the centre of attention.

Now Ariam understood why people said Alexander was a god. He almost worshipped him himself and was determined to meet him. On the third morning he got his chance.

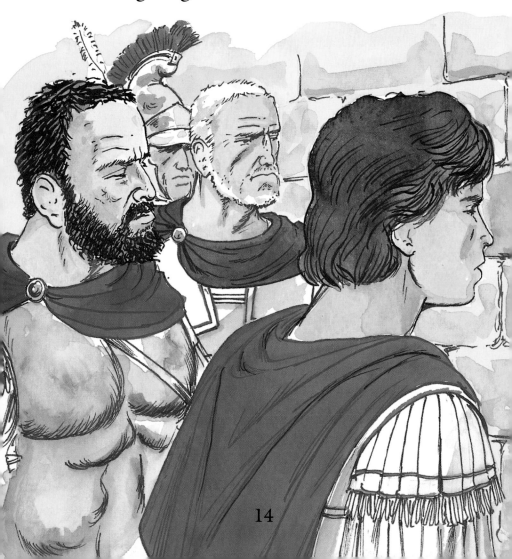

Rounding a corner near the main gate, Ariam found himself facing a group of Macedonian soldiers. Alexander was in their midst. Startled, Ariam stood staring at his hero instead of bowing his head. Alexander gazed directly back at him. Hypnotized by the dark, brilliant eyes, Ariam was unable to look away.

'Who are you?' The king's voice was rapid yet soft.

Ariam opened his mouth but no words came. A soldier grabbed his arm. 'You heard, boy! Who are you?'

With his eyes still on the king's, Ariam said slowly, 'My name is Ariam, sir. I am a cousin of Queen Roxana and...' He paused, unsure what he wanted to say.

'Yes?'

'...and I want to serve you, my lord!' Later, Ariam realized the idea had been growing in his mind for some time without his knowing it.

Alexander flashed him a quick smile. 'Really? How old are you?'

'Almost twelve, my lord.'

'You look older,' Alexander replied, taking in the boy's strong limbs and lively, intelligent face. 'Are you prepared to learn Greek and train with my army?' Ariam nodded. 'And you understand that your life will be very hard?' Ariam nodded again.

'Very well, if your father agrees, report to Craterus in the morning.' He pointed to the soldier holding Ariam's arm.

The man frowned. 'But the boy's not a Macedonian, sir! Not even a Greek!'

'My wife is not a Greek,' Alexander said calmly. 'Try to understand, Craterus. We are building a new world, more broad-minded than the one into which you were born.'

Chapter 3
India!

Baron Pitames had brought up his son
to be tough and independent-minded, so
he was not altogether surprised by Ariam's
decision. Besides, it would be a great
honour to have a son serving so
magnificent a king as Alexander. With
painful tears and promises he knew he
would not be able to keep, Ariam said
goodbye to his family and exchanged the
warm fires of home for the tough training
and rough living of a soldier.

The discipline was fierce, the work hard and the punishments severe. Ariam was not alone, however. That winter Alexander recruited hundreds of other Persian boys. His aim, he said, was to turn them into Greeks as brave as those from distant Macedonia.

Craterus was Ariam's commanding officer. The grizzled veteran of a dozen victories doubted the king's policy. 'A Greek soldier is born', he was fond of saying, 'not made on the training ground.' Some of the young recruits ran away, unable to take his bullying. But not Ariam. Craterus' harshness only increased his determination not to let down his family and to prove himself a worthy servant of the Lord of All Asia.

The following spring, in the year 327BC, Ariam heard that Alexander was about to set out on new conquests. He planned to lead his army through the mountains into India.

India! Ariam knew it only as a land of mystery and fabulous wealth, set on the very edge of the world. In India, he had heard, gold was mined by ants and a one-legged tribe lay on their backs and shaded themselves with their single, huge

feet. More alarming, Indian soldiers rode into battle on the backs of elephants.

To begin with, however, Ariam found India rather disappointing. He was bored by the dusty plains. He saw no gold-mining ants or one-legged tribesmen, and the people fought no better than anyone else. As Alexander advanced, local kings made peace with him or were easily crushed in battle. At least, that is how it was until they met King Porus.

Eighteen months after leaving
Koh-i-noor, Alexander's army entered the
kingdom of Taxila. Its ruler, King Ambhi,
welcomed the invader and offered to help
him in his conquests. In return, he asked
for help in overcoming his neighbour,
King Porus.

Porus' army, Ariam learned, was more
powerful and better organized than any
in India. At its heart was a troop of two
hundred ferocious war elephants.

Chapter 4
The Crossing

Standing at the edge of Alexander's camp
at Haranpur, Ariam looked across the
swollen yellow waters of the River
Hydaspes. On the opposite bank, weapons
glinting in the summer sun, stood the
archers, swordsmen, light cavalry and
chariots of Porus' army. They shouldn't
give us too many difficulties, thought
Ariam – as long as we can reach them.

But that was the problem. The fast-flowing river would be difficult to cross. Even if Alexander's men managed to reach the bank, Ariam realized, they'd never be able to climb it. For there, lined up in a great grey-gold wall, Porus had arranged his war elephants. Armour-clad, tusks tipped with steel knives and with archers perched on wooden platforms on their backs, they were a terrifying sight.

Medius, a young Macedonian officer, came up and stood beside Ariam. 'It's not going to be easy, is it?' he murmured.

Ariam was now a strong and fit young man of almost fourteen. He already had a reputation for intelligence and skill on horseback. Although not yet old enough to fight in battle, he had sometimes been included in scouting parties under Medius' command.

'Not easy at all, sir,' he replied.

'So what would you do?' asked
the officer.

Ariam thought for a moment. 'I
suppose I'd try to find a way round.'

'Just what Alexander thinks,' smiled
Medius. 'He's ordered me to lead a
scouting party upstream to find a
crossing place. Want to join us?'

'Yes, sir!' said Ariam eagerly.

Medius' scouts set out late that afternoon. They rode out of sight of the enemy for a couple of hours, then veered back towards the river. To their disappointment, the bank on their side was steep and rocky. They spread out and tried to find a way down. After searching in vain until it was almost dark, Medius gave up.

As he prepared to lead his men back to
Haranpur, Medius noticed that Ariam was
missing. 'Young fool!' he muttered. 'He
knows he shouldn't...'

Medius' grumbling was interrupted by
the sound of hooves approaching from the
direction of the river. Seconds later Ariam
appeared out of the gloom.

'I've found it, sir!' he panted.

'Found what?'

'A path down to the river.'

'And can the river be crossed there?'

'No problem, sir.' Ariam paused, then added with a grin, 'At least, I'm sure Alexander will manage it.'

Chapter 5
'He Can Do Anything!'

The next morning Medius and his scouts took Alexander to examine the ford for himself. They halted under cover of the trees at the foot of the path and looked across the angry river.

'There's an island in the middle of the stream,' explained Medius. 'We can ferry soldiers to it by boat.'

Alexander frowned. 'And then? How do we get from the island to the opposite bank?'

'We wade across. It's only about fifty paces,' Medius replied.

'It's risky,' said Alexander, leaning his head to one side. 'If the leader gets swept away, the troops will be stuck on the island and the whole plan will fail.'

Ariam could contain himself no longer. Stepping forward, he blurted out, 'Excuse me, sir, but the leader won't get swept away! He can do anything!'

'I didn't ask for advice!' snapped
Alexander, swinging round to see who had
spoken. 'Oh, it's you.' His face softened.
'Ariam from Sogdiana, isn't it?'

'Yes sir.'

Alexander looked at him carefully.
'You've changed, Ariam,' he said, nodding
with approval. 'Almost a soldier now.
Tell me, who is this leader
who can do anything?'

Ariam felt himself blushing with embarrassment. 'You, sir,' he stammered. 'I thought you were going to lead the men across.'

Alexander paused for a few seconds, then turned back towards the river. 'Of course!' he said quietly. 'I will lead the river crossing myself.'

Later, as they were making their way
back up the path to the top of the bank,
Medius drew up his horse alongside
Ariam's and whispered, 'I wouldn't be in
your place, Ariam, for all the gold in India.
If anything goes wrong...'

Nothing did go wrong. While Craterus
distracted the enemy with false attacks
around Haranpur, Alexander shipped a
large force across to the island several miles
upstream. Then, seated on his trusted
war-horse Bucephalas, he plunged into
the swollen river.

Watching from the bank, Ariam saw the water rise to Alexander's feet, then to his knees. Bucephalas staggered on the slippery river bed. For one dreadful moment Ariam thought he would be swept away. But Bucephalas was skilful as well as strong. He regained his footing and was soon safe on dry land.

With a cheer of relief, the men on the island plunged into the river and followed their commander across the river. Before long, thousands of foot soldiers and cavalry men were standing on the opposite bank ready for battle.

Chapter 6
A Trusty Friend

Alexander's crossing took Porus by surprise. To deal with the danger, he divided his army. While one force went to meet Alexander, the other waited on the bank in case Craterus attacked them from behind. It was a serious mistake.

From the opposite bank, Ariam saw Alexander's veterans and their Indian allies sweep aside the band of chariots and cavalry sent against them.

Ariam then galloped furiously back to Craterus' camp to watch the rest of the battle. He arrived to find the Indian king pulling his remaining troops away from the river and arranging them to face Alexander's advance. The war elephants were in the centre of the line.

To Ariam's surprise, Alexander did not order an all-out attack. Instead, he sent his cavalry thundering off to the left. Porus, an able commander, thought he was being surrounded and ordered his cavalry to follow. The skilled Greek horsemen suddenly turned and cut their pursuers to pieces. It was a brilliant move.

At this moment, Ariam noticed Alexander signalling frantically to Craterus. The general waved back and ordered his men to cross the river and attack Porus' army from the rear. The tactic worked perfectly, leaving the elephants no room to charge. Alexander's foot soldiers attacked them at close quarters with huge swords and axes. Driven wild by the pain, the poor beasts stampeded, trampling friend and foe alike.

The battle was over in a few hours. Porus was captured and thousands of his men lay dead on the battlefield. Many Macedonians had been killed, too, and Alexander had suffered a tragic personal loss. Bucephalas, the great war-horse which had been with him since he left Greece, had been gravely wounded and died shortly after the battle.

That evening, to Ariam's surprise, Alexander sent for him. He found his hero sitting in his tent with Craterus. The face of the Lord of All Asia was streaked with tears.

'Tell me, Ariam,' he asked, 'what's the name of the place where we crossed the river?'

'They call it Mangal Dev, sir.'

'From now on it will be known as Bucephala. I will found a city there in memory of a great friend.'

He turned to Craterus. 'Medius tells me this young man found the ford.'

'Yes, I heard that too,' grunted Craterus.

'And he assured me that Bucephalas and I could get across,' Alexander continued. Craterus raised an eyebrow.

The king went on, 'So perhaps, in losing one trusty friend, I have found another?'

Craterus looked at Ariam. 'I was wrong,' he said slowly, a smile spreading across his weather-beaten face. 'Greek soldiers can be made on the training ground after all.'

Glossary

ally a country or person joining with another to help them in war

baron a nobleman

cavalry soldiers who fight on horseback

empire many territories ruled by an emperor

foe enemy

ford a place where a river is shallow enough to be crossed on foot or horseback

Hydaspes the river now known as the Jhelum; a tributary of the River Indus

Parthia a region in the centre of Persia

Persia modern Iran

philosopher a Greek word meaning a 'lover of wisdom'; Greek philosophers studied every aspect of the world and human life

to recruit to get people to join the army

Sogdiana a region in Central Asia, near modern Turkmenistan

to stampede to rush about out of control

tactics the way troops are positioned and moved around during a battle

veteran a soldier who has served in the army for a long time

46